Flossie McFluff

An Irish Fairy

For Róisín, Art, Sal and Igg (EO'B)

For my parents, who instilled and encouraged my love for
books, both in their own way (AD)

Eoin O'Brien has seen foxes, hedgehogs, butterflies and once even a
sparrowhawk in his back garden. He's keeping his eyes open, just in case.

Audrey Dowling is a French artist and illustrator living in County Kilkenny.
She initially pursued a career in the fashion industry in Paris but somehow ended
up in the Irish countryside. Her surroundings inspire her work, as well as folklore
from all cultures, fairy tales and vintage imagery. Her universe is colourful and
narrative, often praised as graceful and poetic.

Acknowledgements

Thanks to all the amazing denizens of The O'Brien Press, particularly the awesome Emer Ryan and Nicola Reddy,
and the incredible Emma Byrne. And to Audrey for elevating my little stories to the level of pure magic. (EO'B)

First published 2021 by The O'Brien Press Ltd,
12 Terenure Road East, Rathgar, Dublin 6, D06 HD27, Ireland.
Tel: +353 1 4923333; Fax: +353 1 4922777
E-mail: books@obrien.ie
Website: www.obrien.ie
The O'Brien Press is a member of Publishing Ireland.

ISBN: 978-1-78849-218-8

Published in
DUBLIN
UNESCO
City of Literature

7 6 5 4 3 2 1
25 24 23 22 21

Printed bound by Drukarnia Skleniarz, Poland.
The paper used in this book is produced using pulp from managed forests.

Flossie McFluff

An Irish Fairy

Written by
EOIN O'BRIEN

Illustrated by
AUDREY DOWLING

THE O'BRIEN PRESS
DUBLIN

Contents

In a deep, leafy wood, by a slow-moving stream,
Where butterflies flutter through golden sunbeams,
Lives a beautiful fairy called Flossie McFluff.
She's tiny and shiny, but Flossie is tough.

She has magical powers, she knows magic words,
And she cares for the trees and the bees and the birds.
Wee Flossie lives high in an ancient oak tree,
And lives for adventure, as we shall soon see …

Pack up Your Picnic

One day, little Flossie was fluttering by,
Singing sweetly along with the birds of the sky.
Then she let out a sound as if someone had bit her,
When she saw that the ground was all covered in litter!

Rubbish piled up on the green forest floor!
Bottles and papers and wrappers and more.
It filled her with fury, this terrible sight;
Her face turned to purple, then red and then white.

So Flossie flew up to the tallest treetop
(Not scary for fairies; there's no chance she'll drop).
She looked all about, up and down, left and right,
Till the litterbugs finally came into sight.

8

'Aha! There you are! Now, prepare to surrender
To Flossie McFluff, the forest defender.
You litterbugs need to be taught a good lesson;
A litter hug should put an end to your messin'!'

A twirl of her wand, and the rubbish rose up
In a cloud, and it followed those messy young pups,
Till it caught them and stuck to their arms and their knees.
'What's happening?' they cried as they tried to get free.

Then Flossie called out in a magical boom,
'*Fáilte* to the forest, there's plenty of room
In our beautiful wood, but be good when you're through.
Pack up your picnic or I'll pick on you!'

Those litterbugs fled, crying out for their Mummy,

While Flossie just laughed as she rolled on her tummy.

Then she turned to the trees and she whispered, 'Don't worry,

Those messers won't do that again in a hurry.'

She watched them run off in a desperate dash
And she said to the oak and the elm and the ash,
'You want to know something? If one thing is true,
Us wee folk are tree folk; we'll look after you.'

The Lonely Banshee

One night lovely Flossie was warm in her nest
With her favourite teddy, all ready for rest,
When a horrible howling came echoing out.
Said Flossie, 'Now, what is that racket about?'

It was poor Wailin' Bridget, the spooky banshee,
Just crying and moaning out under the trees,
So loud and so sad in the darkness so deep.
Flossie knew there was no chance of getting to sleep.

15

So out of her home and up into the air,
It's McFluff to the rescue, anytime, anywhere!
In the dark forest's dreariest corner was lying
Poor Bridget banshee, with her eyes red from crying.

'Oh, nobody likes me!' cried Bridget. 'If only
I'd someone to talk to! I just get so lonely
Out here on my own in the dark in the trees,
But who'd want a friend that's spooky like me?'

'Hang on,' said McFluff, 'I know someone who might!
We'll ask Úna the owl – sure she stays up all night
And she's pale and she's spooky; she'll know what to do.
She's full of too-wit, with a bit of too-woo.'

Before very long, Úna owl drifted by.
Like a great silent shadow she swooped through the sky
And landed right there on a branch of a tree.
Said Flossie, 'Can you help this lonely banshee?'

'No problem,' said Úna. 'I'm so glad you came.
Come join the night chorus; come join in our games.
When it's dark we play blind man's buff under the trees;
When the moon's out, it's spooooky karaoke.'

'Oh my,' cried the banshee, 'that does sound like fun!
And maybe my singing career has begun.'
As Bridget wailed softly, the mice clapped their paws
And the bats flapped their wings and the owls clicked
  their claws.

Now Bridget has plenty of friends in the woods –
All the bats and the badgers, the mice and the toads,
And the foxes and frogs, and they all sing in tune
As sweet Flossie sleeps 'neath the pale yellow moon.

Good as Gold

One morning, as Flossie was brushing her teeth,
She heard her name called from the ground far beneath.
Her leprechaun friend Paddy Potts stood below
With a look on his face full of worry and woe.

'Oh, Flossie, please help me,' said poor Paddy Potts,
'I can't find my gold, I've simply forgot
Where I put it, my magical leprechaun crock.
Was it down by the river, or under a rock,

Or deep in a well? Is it hidden or buried?

Please help me, dear Flossie. I'm terribly worried.'

(A leprechaun knows, from his beard to his britches,

He must guard his gold and look after his riches.)

'Well, Paddy,' said Flossie, 'There's no point in stewing.
Just try to remember the things you were doing.'
'Now, where was I yesterday?' Paddy Potts said.
'I did so much before I went home to my bed.

'I was dancing with butterflies, swimming with frogs,
Then jumping with rabbits, then lunch with hedgehogs.
Then back to my toadstool for dandelion tea.
But my gold isn't there now. Oh, where can it be?'

'Don't worry,' said Flossie, 'I know what to do.
Everything will be fine by the time that we're through.'
She pulled out her wand, and she gave it a jiggle,
A twirl and a twist and a mystical wiggle,

And out of the end, in the blink of an eye,
Came a shower of colours that shot through the sky
Till a beautiful rainbow shone out of the blue,
Curving way overhead till it vanished from view.

'Of course!' said the leprechaun, smiling with glee,
'At the end of the rainbow, that's where it will be!
Where leprechauns keep all their valuable stuff.
What a good friend you are, little Flossie McFluff.'

And Flossie replied, as she giggled with pleasure,
'A good friend's worth more than a leprechaun's treasure.'
Then away Paddy ran to uncover his goods,
At the end of the rainbow, deep in the woods.

So if you go wandering under the trees
And spy a wee twinkle that winks in the breeze,
It could be a sunbeam on some mossy stuff,
Or it might be a fairy called Flossie McFluff.